And Then It Happened
.. 11 ..

AND THEN IT HAPPENED

HAPPENED

•• 11 ••

M & L Wade

Books for Boys

ISBN 9780988115200

Printed in Canada by Hignell Book Printing

Books For Boys Inc.
P.O. Box 87
Strathroy ON N7G 3J1

Table of Contents

Chapter 1

Mama Bear

It was Friday morning and our school was having a raffle to raise money for new playground equipment. Normally, this would be a good thing, but this time the teachers had donated the prizes to be raffled off, and as every student knows, teachers should never be in charge of picking out prizes for kids.

Gordon, Paulo and I entered the gym to look at the prizes that the teachers thought we wanted. Mrs. Hoagsbrith stood proudly beside her prize of a large dictionary. No kids were lined up to buy tickets for that. Our geography teacher was next with a world atlas. Not surprisingly, there was no line-up there either. Our music teacher was raffling off a book called *The History of Wind Instruments*, and the French teacher was hoping to sell tickets for a book called *Popular French Verbs*. In fact, the only teacher who had any kids lined up to buy raffle tickets was the Kindergarten teacher. She had brought a life-sized stuffed bear. The sign in front of her table said, "Win Mama Bear!" Dozens of little kids were lined up to buy tickets for a chance to win Mama Bear.

Disgusted with the prizes, Gordon, Paulo and I sighed and turned to leave the gym.

"Let's get out of here," I said. "There's nothing good. We'll just give the raffle money back to our parents."

Gordon quickly spun around to face me. "Give the money *back*? That's crazy talk!" he shouted. "It would send our parents the wrong message! If we gave the money back," he explained, "the next time we ask our parents for money, they'll laugh and say, *'Ha! Remember that time you thought you needed money for the raffle but you really didn't? Well, this is just like that time,'* and we'll never get any money again. Heck, we *have* to spend this money!"

Paulo and I recognized good logic when we heard it. Turning around, we got in line with the rest of the kids to buy tickets to win the Mama Bear, figuring we could always give it away, or maybe even sell it.

At the end of the day, the tickets were drawn and the prizes were handed out. A little girl in Kindergarten ended up winning the big Mama Bear. It was so big, five other kids had to help her carry it back to her class. The bell rang and we were dismissed from school for the weekend.

Gordon, Paulo and I headed straight to Gordon's house for a quick snack and then we grabbed our fishing gear and bikes, ready to head off for a few hours of fishing. Just as we were about to leave, Gordon's mother came out of the house and gave Gordon her cell phone, saying that she would call him when it was time to come home. Gordon slipped the phone into his pocket and we pedalled off down the road.

On the outskirts of town, we saw the same six little kids from school ahead of us, carrying the big Mama Bear over their shoulders heading to the little girl's house.

"They look exhausted," said Gordon. "Why don't we help them carry the bear the rest of the way?"

We began pedalling toward the kids to help them when a black truck pulled up beside them and came to a stop. Four big high school boys got out of the truck. Gordon, Paulo and I hit the brakes and watched, assuming that *they* were going to help the little kids with the big Mama Bear. Instead, the biggest kid said, "Well, well, well. What have we here?"

"I won this big bear," smiled the little girl. "It's the Mama Bear! We're taking her home to my house."

"Tell me something," grinned the high school boy. "Do bears fly or walk?"

One of the little Kindergarten boys said, "Bears walk! They don't fly!"

The high school boy laughed evilly. "Well, my friends and I are going to teach your bear to fly." He yanked the bear out of the kids' hands and each of the four high school boys grabbed a paw, swinging the bear back and forth, counting, "One, two, three!" On three, they heaved the bear high into the nearest tree where it caught on a branch and stuck. The little kids instantly burst into tears as the boys laughed, jumped into their truck and sped away.

Gordon, Paulo and I quickly pedalled over to the little kids. Gordon stopped them from crying by saying, "Listen. Don't worry. The bad kids are gone, and my friends and I will help you get the Mama Bear down from the tree and carry it safely home."

The tears stopped as quickly as they had started and the nine of us walked over to the tree where the Mama Bear sat high up in the branches. But, try as we might, neither Gordon, Paulo nor I could climb this tree. The lower branches were simply too thin to support us.

"If I could reach that branch, I could climb that tree," said the little girl, surprising us.

"Really?" said Gordon, and he came up with a plan. I got down on all fours and Gordon stood on my back. Paulo lifted the little girl up onto Gordon's shoulders. From here, she was just tall enough to reach the first thin branches of the tree. She easily climbed her way up the tree to where the Mama Bear was stuck. I have to admit, we were all impressed, until the little girl looked down and yelled, "I'm scared up here! I can't get back down!!" She immediately burst into tears.

"Oh, great," sighed Paulo. "Now what do we do?"

To make things worse, her five little friends decided to help out by bursting into tears as well.

"Man, I *never* want to be a Kindergarten teacher," moaned Gordon. "These kids are impossible. What are we going to do now?"

"Well, it was your idea for getting her up into the tree, so you figure it out," said Paulo.

"Yeah," I agreed. "This is all your fault, Gordon." Growing up with Gordon, Paulo and I learned that it was best to blame early, and blame often. Gordon hung his head in shame. He had put a little girl way up into a tree, and now she was terrified to climb back down. *What if she fell?* We had to act fast.

Suddenly Gordon brightened. Reaching into his pocket, he pulled out the cell phone his mother had loaned him.

"Great!" I said. "Just call the police and they can come over with the fire department and get the kid down." Gordon's face darkened and he slid the phone back into his pocket. "I can't phone the police," he said. "We're always in trouble with them. They might think we did this on purpose and call our parents. Then 'Pow!' We'll all be grounded again!"

Paulo and I nodded in agreement. We definitely didn't want trouble with the police. Gordon snapped his fingers. "I got it! I'm gonna phone the radio station and tell them what's going on. Then they can announce it over the radio. Someone listening will hear that a little kid is stuck in a tree and they'll come here with a ladder and get her down."

Paulo and I breathed a sigh of relief. It was perfect. What could possibly go wrong with this plan?

Gordon dialed the radio station and said to the DJ, "Hi. I'm just at the edge of town where the forest starts on

County Road 4. There's a little girl trapped way up on a tree branch next to a big Mama Bear. I was hoping one of your listeners could come over and help...Hello? *Hello??* He hung up," said Gordon, puzzled.

"Did he say anything?" I asked.

"All he said was, *'oh my gosh, yes!'* and then he hung up," repeated Gordon.

"Well, if he said yes, then hopefully he'll announce it. All we have to do is wait for someone to show up," said Paulo.

Gordon, Paulo and I and the five little kids sat under the tree and told the sobbing girl that help was on the way.

Meanwhile, back at the radio station, the DJ had hung up the phone on Gordon and immediately turned to his microphone. Shouting, he told his entire listening audience, "I interrupt this song to announce an emergency. Out on County Road 4, where the forest begins, a huge bear has trapped a little girl in a tree. We need every able-bodied person to get down there as fast as possible to try and save the child from this ferocious bear!"

He did not have to repeat himself. Everyone listening immediately dropped whatever they were doing and rushed to help save the little girl trapped in the tree, about to be eaten by a huge, savage bear. Hunters grabbed their guns, threw them in their pick-up trucks and sped off. Farmers leapt out of their tractors and jumped into their trucks, pitch forks at the ready to do battle with the bear. At the old-age home, doors burst open, and a fleet of electric wheel chairs filled with 90-year old war veterans came pouring out, canes swinging. Even our teacher, Mrs. Hoagsbrith, who had been shopping in town, heard the news over the store's loudspeakers and leapt into her brand new pick-up truck. She, too, began speeding towards County Road 4 to help save the child.

As word spread from person to person, the story got bigger and bigger. When our Police Chief looked out his office window and saw cars and trucks racing by at top speed, ignoring every traffic law, he ran out and bellowed, "What do you people think you're doing?"

One driver yelled back, "Haven't you heard, Chief? A

bunch of bears are attacking kids out on County Road 4!!
It was all over the radio!!"

"Well, go, man! Go!!" encouraged the Chief, running to
his cruiser to join the expanding mob.

*　　*　　*　　*　　*

"Hmmm," I said looking up two minutes later. "What's
that sound?"

"I hear it, too," said Gordon, with a puzzled expression
on his face.

"Look," said Paulo, pointing into the distance. We
squinted and saw a fast-moving cloud of dust way down the
road, getting closer by the second.

"What do you think it is?" I asked.

Seconds later, we found out. Cars, trucks, and police
cruisers came tearing up the road toward us. With brakes
squealing and gravel flying, they came to a crashing halt. A
hundred determined men and women jumped out of their
vehicles.

"There it is!" yelled one man, pointing up the tree. Instantly, hundreds of guns snapped into firing position.

"Don't shoot!" ordered the Police Chief. "You might hit the girl!" All the guns were lowered.

"This fight will have to be hand-to-hand!" someone yelled and everyone charged forward, hoping to be the first up the tree to save the little girl from the bear.

Gordon, Paulo and I and the five little Kindergarten kids were completely ignored as the crowd surged forward. And then it happened. A shiny new pick-up truck came racing onto the scene. The driver tried to swerve to avoid the mob of people, which scattered in all directions. The truck spun around on the gravel and crashed into the tree where the little girl and the Mama Bear were trapped. The crash caused the Mama Bear to come loose. It fell from the branch and toppled down, right into the back of the truck.

"Open fire!!" yelled the Chief, and dozens of guns swung toward the back of the truck and opened fire. Terrified, the driver dove to the floor of the truck for safety as the back of the pick-up truck was riddled with bullets.

Tires were shot, the air hissing out of them loudly, causing the truck to sink down into the gravel. Suddenly, the air was filled with what looked like a sudden snow storm as the bear's white stuffing flew in all directions and rained down on the crowd.

"Cease fire!!" yelled the Police Chief. "I'm going in!" Bravely, he approached the shot-up vehicle and reached into the bed of the pick-up truck. He pulled out the shredded remains of the Mama Bear and held it up.

Sensing that the danger was over, the driver of the truck opened the door and slowly crawled out of the vehicle. Gordon, Paulo and I gasped as we recognized the stunned face of our teacher, Mrs. Hoagsbrith.

Looking at her shot-up truck, she could only mutter, "My truck. My brand-new truck."

"Who on earth said a bear was attacking a little girl?" growled the Chief angrily.

"Let's go!" whispered Gordon to Paulo and me. As we quietly slipped away from the crowd, we heard the sound of a fire truck's siren approaching the scene to get the little girl down from the tree.

"Well," said Gordon when we were safely away from the crowd. "I'm sure glad we had nothing to do with that mess."

"Me, too," I said. "Someone sure is going to be in a lot of trouble."

"Yup," agreed Gordon. "I'd hate to be that DJ when the Chief of Police finds out that he started this whole thing."

That night as we watched the news, we were happy to hear the newscaster announce the day's top story: "Fire crews rescued a little girl from a tree on County Road 4 after reports that she was being chased by a bear. I'm happy to report that no one was hurt, but a pick-up truck and a large stuffed bear were completely destroyed in the incident."

Chapter 2

Expelled!

Gordon, Paulo and I have a rule: Always stay away from trouble. The problem is, trouble doesn't always stay away from us. In fact, trouble seems to chase us around and tackle us when we least expect it. Take yesterday, for example. It was lunchtime, and Gordon, Paulo and I were returning back to school after eating lunch at Gordon's house. As usual, we were minding our own business while we waited for the traffic light to change so we could cross the road. We watched as a mother pushed a baby carriage and dragged her screaming four year old son by the hand through the busy intersection. The kid was really having a fit. In his right hand he held a small red truck, and in his anger, he threw the truck high into the air. As bad luck would have it, our former grade two teacher, Mrs. Campbell, was also crossing the road behind the mother and her children. The toy truck sailed through the air and came crashing down on her nose. It bounced off, hit the traffic light, and then disappeared down a sewer grate. The mother noticed none of this as she struggled to cross the road with her children. Stunned by the pain, Mrs. Campbell fell in the middle of the intersection, blood gushing down her face. Seeing that the traffic light was about to change, Gordon, Paulo and I raced forward to help her. Dodging cars and trucks, we wrapped her arms around our shoulders and helped her to the sidewalk and lowered her to the ground. Gordon pulled a clean towel from his gym bag and tried to slow the blood that was pouring from her nose. Paulo took off his jacket, rolled it up and placed it under her head. I covered Mrs. Campbell with my sweatshirt to keep her warm. Not sure what to do next, we were relieved to see an ambulance and a police car pull up. As they loaded our former teacher into the back of the ambulance, she said in a weak voice, "Tell the principal that I've been injured and that someone will have to cover my class." We promised her that we would. The door slammed shut and the ambulance roared away. Gordon, Paulo and I gathered up our things and continued on our way back to school.

We planned to go straight to the office to report what had happened, but when we got to the school yard, our jaws dropped in surprise. Every kid in the school was playing soccer in the world's biggest soccer match! Instead of 11 kids on each side, there were hundreds of kids on each team. They were screaming and laughing as they ran around the field, and Gordon, Paulo and I wasted no time in joining them. For twenty minutes we raced around the school yard, and when the bell rang, we filed back into class excited, sweaty and out of breath. Everyone was still talking about the wild game.

Mrs. Hoagsbrith quickly quieted us down, and we started our history lesson. At that moment, our principal and several concerned-looking teachers opened our classroom door and said, "Mrs. Hoagsbrith, have you seen Mrs. Campbell? She never returned after lunch. We're getting worried."

"Oh!" Gordon blurted out. "I forgot to tell you! She was hit by a truck!!"

"Wh-what?" asked our principal, shocked.

"Yup, blood everywhere!" I added, trying to be helpful.

Very alarmed, Mrs. Hoagsbrith said, "Well, did the truck at least stop?"

"No!" said Paulo. "It hit a traffic light and disappeared!"

"We were supposed to tell you, but in all the excitement of the soccer game, we forgot." said Gordon. "Sorry."

Now, Mr. Evans had yelled at Gordon, Paulo and me many times in the past, but today was the Guinness world record of yelling.

"You three are the worst boys in the world! A poor teacher is hit by a truck and you can't even remember to report it? Talk about *irresponsible!* I can't stand to even look at you three! I want you out of my school! This is a detention, a suspension and an expulsion all rolled into one! I just wish we could bring back the strap!! And don't come back without your parents. I wanna talk to them. And while you're at it, tell them to bring *their* parents, too!"

Gordon, Paulo and I opened our mouths to explain that we had done our best to help Mrs. Campbell, and that she was going to be all right, but everyone was too mad to even let us speak.

Mr. Evans pointed to the door and said, "I don't want to hear it! *Out!!*"

We packed up our backpacks and headed out of the classroom as teachers and students all shook their heads at us in disgust.

Just as we were about to leave the school yard, a police car pulled up and Mrs. Campbell stepped out of the car. Seeing us, she immediately grabbed Gordon, Paulo and me and pulled us into an embarrassing hug. She showed us the stitches she had gotten across her nose and thanked us over and over for the quick and thoughtful help we had given her. The big police officer stood next to Mrs. Campbell, looking very pleased and proud of us.

"Yup," he said. "In twenty years of policing, I've never heard of kids doing such a good job helping an injured person. I'd be proud to shake your hands." And then it happened. Mr. Evans glanced out of his window and saw Gordon, Paulo and me still in the school yard and talking to a police officer! He came charging out of the school yelling, "Aha! Good work, officer. What did you catch them doing now? Well, I don't even care. Just throw the book at them. I don't want to see them at this school ever again."

"What?" yelled Mrs. Campbell, whom Mr. Evans had failed to notice in his rage. "These boys practically saved my life. I was knocked down in the middle of a busy intersection, and they helped me to the side of the road and gave me first aid until help arrived. These three boys are heroes. They deserve a medal."

"That's right," the police officer said, looking at Mr. Evans and angrily tapping his billy club in the palm of his hand. "Maybe *you're* the one who should be expelled."

Gordon, Paulo and I could see that things were spinning out of control. We knew we had to do the right thing quickly.

"Hey! Whoa. Everyone calm down," soothed Gordon. "There's a simple explanation to all this, and you three adults need to figure out what that explanation is. Meanwhile, until you do, my friends and I have been expelled, so until we officially hear otherwise, we'll be down at the river fishing."

Before Mr. Evans could take back our expulsion, the three of us raced out of the school yard to enjoy our day of freedom.

Chapter 3

Kidnapped!

It was the week before Thanksgiving and our school board was holding a competition between all of its schools to see which one could donate the most cans of food to the local food bank. In the past, whenever any type of competition was held between schools, our school always came in dead last. The teachers all worked hard at encouraging us to bring in canned goods, but the students figured Danglemore Public School would come in dead last again, and if we couldn't win, what was the point? After two days, not one student had donated a single can.

Disappointed with our class's lack of interest in the food

drive contest, Mrs. Hoagsbrith reminded us that it wasn't about winning or losing, but about helping people less fortunate than ourselves. So in order to encourage us, she announced that if every single student in our class brought in *just one can of food*, she would suspend homework the next day. Thrilled by the prospect of a night with no homework, every kid in class brought in *two* cans of food the next morning, just to be on the safe side. Looking at the bulging box of food at the back of the room, Mrs. Hoagsbrith beamed at us and told us how proud she was that we were helping the poor. Every kid beamed back, knowing we were helping *ourselves* to a night with no homework.

So pleased was Mrs. Hoagsbrith with our effort, she extended the deal to the next day as well. If every student brought in one more can of food, she would assign no homework that night as well. So pleased were *we* with the prospect of another night with no homework, every student again brought in two cans the next morning. The food box at the back of the room overflowed.

When the other kids in school found out about Mrs. Hoagsbrith's "canned goods for no homework food drive," they demanded that their teachers do the same. Cans began pouring into the school at an amazing rate. A dangerously high pile of canned goods soon appeared in the gym. It was obvious that our school was devoted to a good cause, and getting out of homework was a *very* good cause indeed. With the lack of homework each night, kids had time to go door-to-door asking their neighbours for canned goods, and the piles of cans soon became an avalanche. The teachers were thrilled that their students were being so generous and that Danglemore Public School might actually win its first-ever competition, and it was all because of Mrs. Hoagsbrith's brilliant idea – which the teachers secretly called the "canned goods for no marking food drive."

Our principal, on the other hand, offered absolutely no encouragement whatsoever. He didn't mention the canned food drive on the morning announcements, and he didn't appear to notice the mountain of cans growing in the gym. For the first time ever, it looked as if Danglemore Public

School might actually stand a chance at winning a competition and Mr. Evans hadn't even noticed.

On the last day of the competition, workers from the school board arrived to collect our canned goods. They took them to the food bank with the cans from all the other schools, counted them, and determined the winner.

After lunch that same day, Mr. Evans excitedly announced a surprise school assembly, and all the classes headed to the gym. The superintendent of our Board was standing on the stage. Speaking into a microphone, he smiled and said, "Well, I never thought this day would come, but Danglemore Public School has actually won the canned food drive competition. You collected more cans than all the other schools put together! I don't know how you did it, but I am proud of you! Danglemore Public School is number one!" All the students and teachers cheered. The superintendent then reached into a box and held up a large, shiny coffee mug. "This is a very expensive, 24-karat gold coffee mug," he continued. "It is my pleasure to present this mug to your principal for his outstanding effort in leading your school to an amazing victory!" The gym fell silent. No one cheered. Everyone knew that it was *Mrs. Hoagsbrith* that had led the outstanding effort. She, not Mr. Evans, had encouraged us to bring in cans, and the other teachers had followed her lead. Mr. Evans hadn't even donated a *single can*, much less led us to victory!

The entire school turned to look at Mrs. Hoagsbrith, who sat staring straight ahead at the stage, a tight smile on her face. We figured that Mr. Evans would do the right thing. We thought he would accept the expensive mug and then turn around and call Mrs. H. up on to the stage and give the mug to her. And then it happened.

Mr. Evans leapt out of his chair and ran across the stage to grab the 24-karat gold mug. "I won! I won!" he chanted, doing a silly dance. He clutched the expensive mug to his chest, and then, collecting himself, he stepped up to the microphone and said, "I like to think it's all about leadership. I have been at this school for many years now, and the teachers see me as their natural leader. They look to me for guidance. And when I heard about those poor unfortunate hungry people, I just knew we had to help them. And that's why I deserve this fine mug. Perhaps I should send a large picture of myself to the food bank so that everyone can see the man who helped contribute to such a good cause."

I turned and saw Mrs. H. rolling her eyes. The superintendent ended the assembly, and we headed back to our classrooms.

When we got there, we all began complaining to Mrs. H. We said it was the students who did the hard work of collecting the cans, and it was the teachers who had encouraged us. But mostly, we said, if it hadn't been for Mrs. Hoagsbrith, our school never would have won. The principal did absolutely *nothing*, and he was getting all the credit *and* the expensive mug. When we settled down, our teacher explained that it wasn't important who got the credit. The important thing was that hundreds of hungry people now had lots to eat, thanks to all of our effort. "Now take out your math books," she finished, "and let's get some work done."

Gordon, Paulo and I looked at each other. We were all thinking the same thing; Mrs. Hoagsbrith was a pretty good teacher, but she sure knew nothing about life. In the real world, it made a *great* deal of difference who got the credit.

At recess, we found out that the other classes felt the same way. We all watched as Mr. Evans strolled around the playground, proudly sipping coffee from his new gold mug.

"He sure is proud of that mug," I said.

"Yup," said Paulo. "He sure is."

"And listen to him brag!" said Gordon with disgust. "Taking all the credit for our victory is bad enough, but the man never even brought in a single can of food!"

"There's nothing we can do about that now," I said. "The contest is over."

"I'm not so sure about that," said Gordon. "Food banks are always accepting food. I think he should be made to donate fifty cans himself."

"There's no way he'll do that!" scoffed Paulo.

"Oh, yeah?" said Gordon. "I've got a plan..."

When the school bell rang at the end of the day, Gordon, Paulo and I were the first kids outside. We ran to the side of the school where the principal's office was located. Through the open window we saw it - the expensive 24-karat gold coffee mug sitting on his desk. Reaching through the window, Gordon grabbed the mug and stuffed it in his backpack. We took off, heading for Gordon's house for the next stage in the plan.

First, Gordon filled the principal's prized mug with water and set it on the ground. Then he whistled for his dog Chopper. Just as the dog was about to dip his long tongue into the mug for a drink, I snapped his picture with a camera. It was great! The picture showed a dog about to drink from the mug. On the back of the picture we wrote, "If you don't want your mug to be turned into a dog's water dish, you must donate fifty cans of food to the food bank immediately."

The next day we arrived at school early and slid the picture under the door of the principal's office.

During announcements, Mr. Evans angrily shouted that someone had stolen his prized mug. If anyone knew who stole it, they were to report immediately to his office to tell him. Mrs. Hoagsbrith instantly looked at Gordon. Narrowing her eyes, she asked, "Gordon, did you steal the principal's mug?"

Gordon looked shocked. Placing his hand over his heart, he said, "Mrs. H., I can honestly say that I did not *steal* Mr. Evans' mug."

At recess, Paulo asked Gordon how he could lie to the teacher like that.

"What?" cried Gordon. "I didn't lie to the teacher. I didn't steal that mug. I *kidnapped* it. She never asked if I *kidnapped* the mug. I can honestly say that I didn't steal that mug." Paulo and I grinned at Gordon's cleverness.

The next day, Mr. Evans failed to bring in the fifty cans of food, so we slid another picture under his door. This time, the mug was shown hovering above a toilet bowl, about to be dipped into the water like a huge ladle. On the back of the picture we wrote, "You must now donate *one hundred* cans to the food bank, or the mug gets it!"

When Mr. Evans discovered the latest ransom note, he ranted and raved over the announcements once again. He said that not only would he suspend the guilty student who had taken his mug, but he would suspend the student's teacher as well!"

Again, Mr. Evans failed to bring in any cans the next day. We slid a final picture under his door. This time, the picture showed the prized mug about to be hit by a hammer. On the back it said, "This is your last chance. You must now donate *two hundred* cans to the food bank, or say good-bye to the mug. This is your final warning."

During morning announcements, we waited for our principal to explode, but instead, he quietly read the announcements. When he was done, our class watched through the window as Mr. Evans got into his car and drove away. An hour later, he returned, and we watched as the principal carried in box after box of canned goods. At lunch, someone from the food bank came to collect the two hundred cans and to thank Mr. Evans for his surprise donation.

Satisfied, we snuck the principal's prized mug back into his office the next morning. After lunch that same day when we filed in from recess, we were delighted to see the 24-karat gold mug sitting on Mrs. Hoagsbrith's desk.

Chapter 4

The Halloween House

Like most kids, Gordon, Paulo and I take our trick-or-treating very seriously. Our goal was always the same as every other kid's: To go to as many houses and get as much candy as possible. However, every year, something goes horribly wrong, and we end up with no candy at all. We spent one year lost in a cornfield going in circles until it was too late to trick-or-treat. Another year, our candy was accidently dumped in the river, along with the three of us. Year after year, it was always the same - by the end of the night, we had no candy.

"This year," Gordon declared, "it will be different. I have a great plan. Instead of trick-or-treating as many houses as possible, we need to trick-or-treat the same house over and over."

"Well, that would be a good idea, but won't the person handing out the candy recognize us coming back over and over?" asked Paulo.

"Ha! I already thought of that," said Gordon. "We can print different Halloween masks for free on the computer. We simply cut out the eyes, add some string, and tada! A different mask every time. And the best part is this...the house we are going to trick-or-treat over and over is *the house!*"

Paulo and I grinned. *The house!* Every kid in town knew about *the house*. At the mere mention of *the house*, kids eyes glassed over and they began to drool uncontrollably. *The house* was owned by a little old lady who gave out the best Halloween treats in town. Every year, she gave out the same thing: a big brown paper bag with her name and address written on the outside. Inside the bag was a can of pop, four bags of chips, four chocolate bars and a handful of candy and gum. Gordon, Paulo and I licked our lips and grinned at each other. It wouldn't take many trips to *the house* to completely fill up our pillowcases.

Two days before Halloween, we began printing masks off the computer. We printed monsters, zombies, firefighters, and police masks. We continued printing until we had enough different masks to put our plan into action.

The next night was Halloween. As soon as it got dark, we headed straight for *the house* and rang the bell, wearing the first of our masks. When the little old lady opened the door, she smiled and said, "Oh, what scary zombies! Here you go, kids." She dropped a heavy brown bag into each of our pillowcases. With shouts of 'thank you,' we pretended to head to the next house, but as soon as her door was closed, we doubled back to where we had hidden our masks and put on mask number two.

In half a minute we were back ringing her doorbell again. This time the little old lady opened the door and grinned, "My, what brave firefighters!" She dropped three more brown bags into our pillowcases and closed the door.

Over and over we performed our trick and soon our pillowcases were bulging.

"Wow! That was fast!" I said.

"Yeah!" said Paulo. "I'll bet we just beat the Guinness World Record for filling a pillowcase on Halloween."

"And we have one more mask left," said Gordon. Although our pillowcases were full and the brown candy bags were almost spilling out, we put on our last masks and rang the doorbell one more time. The little old lady opened the door and we called out, "trick-or-treat!" Much to our surprise, the old lady didn't just smile, she stepped outside and herded us into her house.

"Policemen masks!" she exclaimed. "Those are the best costumes I've seen all night! It's so nice to see young boys showing such respect for the law by dressing up as policemen. Harold!" she yelled, turning towards the living room where we could hear a TV. "Come and see these costumes! You'll just love them!"

Turning back to Gordon, Paulo and me, she said proudly, "Harold is my son. He came over for dinner before heading off to work. He's the town's Chief of Police." I instantly broke into an icy cold sweat.

The Chief of Police strolled into the room and grinned when he saw our costumes. "I am so proud to see kids dressed up as our town's finest," he said, giving Gordon a friendly pat on the back. "Before you go, I'd like to get a picture of the four of us together. I'll bet the local paper would be interested in printing it. Get the camera, mother."

"Uh, that's OK." said Gordon nervously as we inched toward the door. "It's getting late and we have to be going."

"It'll only take a second," insisted the Chief of Police, blocking our way. And then it happened. As his mother pointed her camera at us, the Chief quickly leaned forward and swept Gordon, Paulo and me into his outstretched arms. The sudden motion took us by surprise and caused us to drop our overstuffed pillowcases. Dozens of brown labeled bags of candy spilled out onto the floor.

"Well, well, well," said Chief of Police, no longer smiling. "Been playing tricks on my dear sweet mother, have you? Well, I have a little trick for you boys. It's called *'Take Back the Candy and Call your Parents.'* I hope you enjoy it!"

Chapter 5

The Grinch

It was the first Saturday in December. Many people had put up their Christmas decorations, and Gordon, Paulo and I decided to take a walk to some of the richer areas of town to see the displays. As usual, most of the homes were beautifully decorated with every Christmas decoration imaginable, and thousands of twinkling lights were waiting to be turned on at night. There was, however, one exception; the largest house on the richest street in town didn't have a single decoration. No lights, no wreath on the door. Nothing. As we continued on to see the next house, a man's voice called to us from the front door of the undecorated house.

"Hey, would you boys like a job?"

We turned and saw the man on his front porch.

"Maybe," said Gordon, as we walked up the driveway. "What do we have to do?"

"My name is Mr. Karloff," the man said, introducing himself. "This street is famous for its holiday decorating contests, and every holiday, my house wins those competitions. I've won prizes for New Year's, Valentine's Day, Groundhog Day, St. Patrick's Day, Labour Day, Halloween and Thanksgiving. But this year I'm too busy to put up my Christmas decorations. I've just been called into work, and the contest judging is tonight. I'd like you boys to decorate my house. It will take the three of you all day, and I'll give you three hundred - that's one hundred each."

Gordon, Paulo and I looked up at the steep, tall roof. It was snow covered and looked dangerously slippery. One slip, and you could fall to your death. We knew our mothers would kill us if they saw us on such a dangerous roof. Acting responsibly, Gordon, Paulo and I looked up and down the street. Not a mother in sight!

"We'll do it!" Gordon said.

Great!" said Mr. Karloff. He opened his garage door and showed us the piles of decorations, stacked and labelled in boxes for every holiday of the year. There were boxes for New Year's, Valentine's Day, Groundhog Day, St. Patrick's Day, Labour Day, Thanksgiving and Halloween. A large corner of the garage was filled with boxes labeled *Christmas*. "Yes," repeated Mr. Karloff. "I win the contest for every holiday. In life, winning is everything. Beating other people is the most important thing. I'm a lawyer, and I should know. No one gets the better of me." The lawyer pulled out a drawing of his house and yard. Gordon, Paulo and I leaned over to get a better look. The instructions for how to decorate Mr. Karloff's house were laid out in fine detail. There were many pages of directions telling us exactly how he wanted each decoration and light set up.

The man went back inside, leaving Gordon, Paulo and me with the huge job of decorating his house.

Taking the ladder out of the garage, we leaned it up against the chimney. We decided to start decorating the dangerous roof first while we were fresh. It took all of our effort to get the giant sleigh onto the slippery roof, but after fifteen minutes, it was finally in place. Gordon, Paulo and I leaned against the chimney, trying to catch our breath and plan our next move.

"Do you hear something?" I asked.

"I think it's just the guy's phone," said Paulo. "Listen. We'll hear him talking." Huddling around the chimney, we did what any normal kids would do. We quietly eavesdropped.

We heard Mr. Karloff say, "Hello? Hi, Dave. Glad to hear from you. Yeah, I'll be in to work in a few minutes. Guess what? I met some really dumb kids today." Gordon, Paulo and I smiled at each other. We knew a lot of kids like that.

"Yup," continued the lawyer. "They're on my roof right now." Gordon, Paulo and I frowned at each other. "I'm tricking them into putting up all my Christmas decorations for free. I told them I'd give them a hundred each, but I never said a hundred *dollars*. I just said a hundred. So after they spend the whole day decorating my house, I'm going to give each dumb kid a piece of paper with the words 'a hundred' written on it. I'll win the best decorated house again, and it won't cost me a thing! Anyway, I gotta go and check on those dumb kids."

We heard Mr. Karloff hang up the phone and we scrambled down the ladder. Gordon said he was going to tell the lawyer what a jerk he was and we were going to quit, but before Gordon could say anything, Mr. Karloff started speaking.

"There you are, boys. I'm off to my office. I should be home just before dark, in plenty of time to watch the judges award me first prize again. After all, winning is everything."

Suddenly, a new thought came to Gordon. "Okay," he said. "Let me just make sure I've got this straight. At the end of the day, you're going to give us a hundred each?"

"That's right," grinned the lawyer. "A hundred each."

Gordon grinned back. "It's a deal." The lawyer shook our hands, got in his car, and drove away.

Before Paulo and I could say anything, Gordon said, "Ha! He thinks he's tricked us! Well, we'll show him who's dumb. The only prize he's going to win is the World's *Worst* Decorated House when we get through with it." Gordon told us his plan, and we all grinned. It was devious and dirty. *Yes,* I thought. *One day Gordon might be a lawyer, himself.*

First, we carried up a box of St. Patrick's Day decorations, and put eight tiny leprechauns in front of the sleigh. In the sleigh we put not Santa, but a life-size Grim Reaper in a black robe, pointing a bony hand toward the leprechauns. On the front lawn, we put up the rest of the lawyer's Halloween decorations. Witches and skeletons chased Christmas elves around the yard. The elves looked like they were running for their lives! We saved the best for last. In the middle of the yard, we laid the life-size Santa Claus on the ground and folded his hands over his chest. We took a tombstone out of the Halloween box and placed it at his head. It read, "Rest In Peace." Lastly, with his Christmas lights, we were supposed to write *Merry*

Christmas! Instead, we shaped the strings of lights to say *I Hate Christmas!*

"Hey, look," Paulo said, pointing up the street. "They've started the judging." We noticed the mothers on the street taking their children around to view all the decorations. There was tremendous holiday spirit as the festive crowd made its way from house to house. Home owners handed out hot chocolate, candy canes and small presents to the children. There was holiday music, singing and dancing. The judges made their way from house to house taking notes.

Gordon, Paulo and I put away the last of the boxes and joined the crowd as it slowly made its way to the lawyer's house. At last we reached it. The music, singing and dancing stopped. Mothers stared open-mouthed and little kids began to cry as they noticed the dead Santa on the front lawn. And then it happened. Mr. Karloff returned from work and pulled into his driveway, not even looking at the decorations, so certain that he would win the contest again this year. He rolled down his window and smiled at the judges, "Hey, folks. I guess you're here to award me first place again." The lawyer's car was immediately surrounded by an angry mob of mothers, pointing at the words spelled out in lights and chanting, "He hates Christmas! He hates Christmas!" They began rocking his car back and forth and banging on it with their fists. The terrified lawyer looked up and saw for the first time what we had done with his decorations. He tried to talk his way out of it by saying, "I didn't do this! I hired some dumb boys to decorate my house, and this is the mess they made!!"

Angry mothers pointed at the steep, slippery roof. "He made some poor boys climb up on the dangerous roof. He hates Christmas, and he hates boys!" The crowd began rocking his car even harder.

Seeing his chance, Gordon yelled out, "And he hasn't even paid us yet!" The angry mothers took up a new chant: "Pay the boys! Pay the boys!!"

Gordon, Paulo and I stuck our hands into the car through the window and the angry lawyer reluctantly handed us each a crisp hundred dollar bill. "You think you're smart, don't you?" he snarled quietly through clenched teeth.

Grinning at each other, Gordon, Paulo and I took the money and said nothing in return. As we walked away from the car, several mothers said, "What did he just say to you?"

Gordon grinned at me and then turned to face the women. "He said that you were the dumbest bunch of neighbours he's ever had."

We headed home with our money, leaving Mr. Karloff to face an even angrier crowd.

Chapter 6

Just Five Minutes

It was a cold January day and we had just come in from recess and taken our seats. Mrs. Hoagsbrith raised her hand to quiet us all down. "Now, class," she said. "A safety inspector from the school board has arrived to check the outside of the building, and as the principal is sick today, it is my job as senior teacher to show him around the school. It should just take five minutes. The problem is, there is no spare teacher to watch you right now. Can I count on you to behave for *just five minutes* by yourselves?"

We rolled our eyes. Geez! Who did she think we were? A bunch of grade 1s? Of course we could behave for just five minutes without a teacher watching us!!

"Excellent," said Mrs. H., not waiting for a reply. "I knew I could count on you. Take out a book and do five minutes of silent reading. And please," she added as she hurried out of the room, "don't let me down."

For the next five minutes we were the best behaved class in the world. We all read in absolute silence. Glancing at the clock, Gordon said, "Hey, look! Five minutes are up. Mrs. H. was supposed to be back by now and she's not. I feel so let down! She said she'd be gone for just five minutes, and where is she?? We trusted her and she didn't come back! Silent reading is over. Let the games begin!"

Our class went from the world's best behaved class to the world's worst behaved class in five seconds flat. While Paulo and I played catch with a small football, several girls in the back of the class started doing gymnastics. A group of boys practised walking on their hands up and down the aisles, while another group of kids drew funny pictures on the chalkboard. Paper airplanes whizzed around the room and a wrestling match broke out in a corner. At the front of the room, a burping contest began. Six kids raced back and forth on wheeled computer chairs in a relay race. For ten minutes, the noise level grew until we sounded like an angry mob at a soccer game. And then it happened. The room suddenly went silent. I spun around to see Mrs. Hoagsbrith standing in the doorway, hands on hips and staring tiredly around the room. The football bounced off my head and rolled away. Every kid froze.

Mrs. Hoagsbrith stepped into the classroom, and in an exhausted voice she sighed, "All right, everyone, take your seats. Gordon, come over here and take off my coat." Gordon stepped forward and took off the teacher's coat. Mrs. H. then slumped down into a chair and said, "Gordon, take off my boots." Reluctantly, he bent down and pulled off the teacher's boots. "Okay, now my hat and gloves," she said. Gordon removed Mrs. H's hat and gloves. "Now, Gordon," said Mrs. Hoagsbrith sternly, "if I *ever* catch you parading around the classroom in my winter clothes again, imitating me, you'll be sent to the office for the rest of the day!"

Chapter 7

Spring Vacation

Every year our school is closed for one week for Spring Vacation and every year, Gordon, Paulo and I spend a couple of days on a father/son ice fishing trip. Now this wasn't the usual ice fishing, where you fished on a cold, windy lake next to an open hole. No, for this trip, our dads would rent a large heated ice hut. It had a small kitchen and bunks to sleep on at night. We knew our dads enjoyed the trip as much as we did, because the moment we arrived, they'd open up their thermoses, toast each other, and get happier and happier as the day went on, even if we weren't catching any fish. Exhausted by the good times, our dads would tire out early, leaving Gordon, Paulo and me to spend the evening listening to the hockey game on the radio while they snored in the background. There's nothing we loved more than this yearly ice fishing trip.

This year, however, was going to be different. Our mothers got together and sat Gordon, Paulo and me down and said they felt that we were growing up too fast and that they wanted to have a *mother*/son vacation this year. They would let us boys decide.

Gordon's mother said, "You boys can go ice fishing with your dads, *or* you can come on a week-long cruise with us. We know this will be a hard decision for you to make, but —"

Gordon's mother got no further. Gordon, Paulo and I leapt up, knocking over our chairs, yelling, "Cruise! Cruise! We want to go on the cruise with you!!"

Paulo's mother said, "What about your annual ice fishing trip with your dads?"

"We hate ice fishing!!" we lied. "We only go to keep our dads happy. Take us on the cruise ship! The girls can go ice fishing with our dads." Ice fishing *was* lots of fun, but it couldn't compare to a week-long cruise down in the sunny south.

*   *   *   *   *

Just before Spring Break, our mothers took Gordon, Paulo and me out of school a day early and we flew south to board a huge luxury cruise ship called *Good Times*. Gordon, Paulo and I couldn't wait. We had heard that the ship had six different swimming pools, wild water slides and a rock climbing wall open twenty-four hours a day. There were eight restaurants and an all-you-can-eat ice cream bar, all for free. This was going to be the greatest spring vacation ever!

At one o'clock sharp, *Good Times* blasted its horn and slowly made its way towards the open sea. The day was sunny and hot, and there wasn't a single cloud in the brilliant blue sky.

A steward showed us where our cabins were: Mothers in one room and Gordon, Paulo and I in another. Our cabin was on deck D, number 713. Gordon, Paulo and I quickly threw our bags in our room, changed into our bathing suits and ran up on deck to start a week of pure fun. We headed straight to the water park, but we didn't get far. At the entrance, we were stopped by a big security guard. "And just where do you think you're going?" he asked in a deep voice.

"To the water park," said Gordon. "Is this the right spot?"

The guard chuckled. "I'm afraid not, boys. This is an adult only ship. The pools, game room, movie theatres and the water park are off limits to kids at all times. The children's area is below deck. I'll have one of my men escort you there."

We were led down a long dark passageway deep below deck. The security guard stopped in front of a windowless door and pulled out a key. Unlocking the door, he said, "*This* is the children's area."

Gordon, Paulo and I stepped inside the dingy room and stared. There were ten or so other kids sitting at desks with sad expressions on their faces. Without speaking to one another, we turned to run, but it was too late. The security guard slammed the door shut, and we could hear the key turning in the lock on the outside. We were trapped!! Gordon, Paulo and I turned and looked at each other. We knew exactly what this room was - a dungeon, also known as ... *a classroom!!*

The woman at the front turned to us and smiled. "Welcome, boys. I'm Mrs. Black. I will be your teacher for the next week. Now please take your seats. We are just about to start art class. You're in luck! Today, we are going to make sock puppets!!" She beamed at her class, thrilled to be bringing us this news.

Several long hours later, the security guard returned to escort all the kids back to their cabins. As we made our way back up to the top deck, we stared longingly as several adults strolled by with triple-scoop ice cream cones in one hand and fancy drinks with umbrellas in them in the other. We could hear laughter and squeals of delight as adults slid down the water slides and splashed into the cool water below. "Cannonball!" someone shouted, jumping into a crystal clear swimming pool and sending up a huge spray of water. Further along the deck, we saw a line-up for the air-conditioned theatres and drooled as the smell of fresh popcorn wafted out towards us.

"Here you go," said the security guard when we reached room 713. As he turned to leave, Gordon said, "Well, at least we'll be at the first port of call soon. *Then* we can get off this ship and have some fun."

"Oh, no!" corrected the security guard quickly. "This is an *adult only* vacation. Kids aren't allowed to leave the ship. You have to stay in your rooms when we're in port. But don't worry. The kitchen will be serving healthy meals, and sometimes the TV in your room gets *three* channels."

Closing the door behind us, Gordon threw his sock puppet against the wall while Paulo snapped on the TV. The security guard hadn't lied. We did get three channels, but none of them spoke English. We were doomed.

"That's it!" Gordon said angrily. "This is the worst vacation in the world. When this ship docks, let's sneak off and have some fun. Then we'll sneak back on before anyone even knows we've been gone. What could possibly go wrong?"

Gordon is right, I thought. *What could go wrong? And if something does, so what? What can they do to us? Send us back to make more sock puppets or lock us in our cabins?*

"Count me in!" I said, and Paulo quickly agreed.

Several hours later, the ship docked at the first port of call, a beautiful island with sandy white beaches and swaying palm trees. Our mothers stopped by the cabin to check in on us. They apologized, saying that they had no idea that this was an adult only cruise when they booked it, but at least is was better here than being stuck in an ice fishing hut for a week, wasn't it?

Before we could answer, they hurried off to enjoy the first port of call. We waited a full hour for all the adults to make their way off the ship. Then Gordon, Paulo and I cracked open our door, checking carefully for ship security, and tiptoed down the hall to the gangway. With a last look over our shoulders, we sprinted off the ship and onto the island.

The island was great! We spent hours exploring everything it had to offer: the tourist shops, the street vendors, and the beautiful beaches. No one seemed to notice that we were just kids. At midnight, we decided that it was time to sneak back on the ship. *It was going to be a good trip after all,* I thought to myself. *Enjoy the islands by night and sleep all day in our cabin!*

We walked to where all the cruise ships were docked until we found our ship - the *Good Tymes*.

"There it is," said Gordon, pointing. I glanced up and read the name on the side of the ship.

"The *Good Tymes*," I said. "And that's just what we're going to have from now on."

When no one was looking, we dashed up the gangway and snuck back aboard. When we arrived at our room, we were surprised to find that our key didn't work in the lock.

"Great," muttered Paulo. "We're locked out!"

"It's a warm night," said Gordon. "Let's just sleep up on deck and our mothers can get us a new key tomorrow."

We followed Gordon to the top deck, found three lounge chairs and drifted off to sleep. Just before I nodded off, I could feel the ship begin to move and make its way towards the next port of call.

Early the next morning, we awakened and headed off to our mothers' cabin to tell them about our key. We knocked on their door, but there was no answer. It was then that someone tapped on my shoulder and said something in a language I didn't understand.

"What?" I asked, turning to find Gordon, Paulo and myself surrounded by several security guards. The man repeated his question but we could not understand his language.

"Speak English," said Gordon. The guards spoke in a universal language by grabbing the three of us by the collar and marching us to find the captain of the ship.

The guards and captain spoke in their language for a few minutes and then the captain turned and spoke to us in English.

"My security team has discovered you three stowaways.

I am going to have you locked up immediately."

"Ha!" laughed Gordon, reaching into his pocket and pulling out his ship pass. "Maybe *you'll* be locked up for not being able to tell the difference between paying customers and stowaways."

The captain took our tickets and adjusted his glasses as he read them. "This is no good," he said. These passes are for our sister ship, the *Good Times*." He pointed to a deck chair. "Notice the spelling of this ship's name. You are on board the *Good Tymes*, not the *Good Times*."

"OH, NO!" we shouted, as the realization of what we had done sunk in. We had snuck onto the wrong ship!!

"I guess you'll have to turn this ship around, huh?" asked Gordon.

The captain laughed out loud. "Turn this ship around? Your ship is half a day away. It would cost over a hundred thousand dollars in fuel to turn this ship around and bring you back to your ship."

"Well," I said hopefully. "We can catch up with our ship at the next port of call."

"There will be no more ports of call for the *Good Tymes*, I'm afraid. This ship is heading for Europe."

Europe! I thought to myself. *That sounds far away.*

"Wait here." The captain marched away, leaving the three of us with our guards. In a half hour, he returned. "Good news," he smiled. "I have contacted your mothers on our sister ship and explained the situation. A fishing boat called the *Sea Cruise* will be passing by us in a couple of hours. You three will be placed onboard, and in five days, it will arrive at the same port as the *Good Times*. You will meet your mothers there."

Relieved that everything was going to work out, we thanked the captain and sat down on some nearby deck chairs to wait for the fishing boat to come and pick us up.

"This is turning out better than I thought," said Gordon. "I can't wait to get on that fishing boat! We can help the crew reel in some giant ocean fish. Maybe we'll even catch a shark!"

Caught up in Gordon's excitement, Paulo and I began to look forward to getting on the *Sea Cruise* and catching some real fish. This would beat ice fishing any day!

Hours later, a rusty old boat drew up alongside the *Good Tymes*. Curious, we leaned over the rail and stared at it.

"Man, what a dump," exclaimed Paulo.

"I'm surprised they let that thing sail on the ocean. It looks like it's half rusted away," I agreed.

"And get a whiff of it!" said Gordon.

To our shock, the captain approached us and said, "OK, boys. Here's your ride. Grab hold of these ropes and we'll lower you down to the fishing boat."

Before we could open our mouths to protest, the security guards heaved us over the side of the *Good Tymes* and we landed on the rusted deck of the *Sea Cruise*. A large hairy, sweaty man greeted us.

Looking up, Gordon said, "Hi! Can you tell the captain that we're here and that we'd like to be shown to our rooms? Also, if we could get a sandwich or maybe a hamburger, that would be great. We've had a rough morning."

I would know this man for the next five days and this

was the first and only time I ever saw him laugh. When he finished, he clenched his jaw tightly around his cigar and growled, "I *am* the captain. This is a working boat. There *are* no cabins. The crew sleeps on deck at night and works by day. You three swabs are crew. Did you think we were going to let you sail for *free?* This ain't no pleasure cruise. Now get to work!"

We were herded to an assembly line filled with sweaty men and women, none of whom spoke English. Millions of three inch sardines were dumped on a conveyor belt, and it was our job, along with eveyone else, to cut off the heads and tails as the fish rolled past us. The sardines were then taken away to be canned, and the heads and tails were dumped into a bin marked 'cat food.'

We worked under the blazing sun for fourteen hours a day and slept ten hours a night on deck. The food was free – all you can eat sardines for breakfast, lunch and supper.

By the end of the first day, we were covered head to foot in fish scales and slime. Exhausted, we collapsed on deck that night with the other workers. By the third day, salt spray from the ocean had rotted off most of our clothing. We were burnt from the sun and our skin was blistering and red. By the fifth day, we were a total mess. Five days of non-stop fish cleaning and a diet of sardines had turned us to skin and bones.

Finally, at the end of the day, our fishing boat pulled into port alongside the Good Times. The captain told us that our mothers were expecting us at the restaurant around the corner. Gordon, Paulo and I were a little worried about seeing our mothers. We figured they would burst into tears when they saw the condition we were in after five days on the fishing boat. They would feel so guilty they would probably hug and kiss us and embarrass us to death.

When we spotted our mothers at the table, we almost didn't recognize them. They looked relaxed and happy. They were wearing new clothes and had fresh hair styles. Their fingernails and toenails were painted. Being on vacation without any kids made them look ten years younger. They barely looked up when we arrived at their table.

"Oh, there you are!" my mother said. "Back from your little fishing boat adventure already? Did you catch lots of fish?"

And then it happened. Gordon's mother said, "Have a seat boys. I just ordered you the special of the day – all you can eat sardines. You'll have to eat quickly, though. Our flight home leaves in an hour, and you have to be back at school tomorrow."

Chapter 8

Get Well Soon

Our entire class was smiling as we left school on Friday afternoon. It had been the best week of school ever! No homework in the evenings and no homework assigned for the weekend. Our teacher, Mrs. Hoagsbrith, had taken the week off to have a small operation. The substitute teacher that arrived on Monday had been a nervous looking young man. He introduced himself to us as Mr. West and told us that he had just finished teachers' college last week. We were the first class he had ever taught. The class looked at each other and smiled. We couldn't believe our good luck! A brand new teacher to break in!! No one was surprised when Gordon's hand immediately shot into the air.

"Yes?" said Mr. West pointing at Gordon.

"Sir," said Gordon. "You may have noticed that my desk is right next to your desk. Our desks are actually touching. Well, the reason for that is because I am the official teacher's helper. So anything you want to know, just ask me."

"Wow! A teacher's helper!" smiled Mr. West. "That would be great. Like I said, this is my very first day of teaching."

In no time at all, Gordon had talked Mr. West into believing that our class got gym every day, an extra recess every morning, and most importantly, he convinced him that Mrs. Hoagsbrith did not believe in homework on week nights or on weekends.

Five beautiful days later, as I walked home from school with Gordon on Friday, I asked him if he felt guilty for tricking the new teacher like that.

"Guilty?" said Gordon, surprised. "*He's* the one that should feel guilty. He must not have been paying attention in teachers' college when they taught the difference between class *helpers* and class *clowns*. I certainly hope he learned something this week."

With no homework to do, Gordon, Paulo and I got together to explore in the woods on Saturday morning. Several hours later, while biking home, we spotted a snake sunning itself on a rock. We slammed on our bike brakes. A snake was a very useful animal. Whenever we found one, we captured it and brought it home to show our mothers. We always asked if we could keep it as a pet, secretly knowing our mothers would say NO. When our mothers finished yelling at us for bringing a snake into the house, we would put on our "sad faces" and walk slowly away. This, we had learned, made our mothers feel sorry for us and they often said yes to any other requests we might have, such as giving us money to go buy ice cream. We really didn't want the snake for a pet anyway, but our mothers never seemed to catch on to this trick no matter how many times we pulled it. They were just relieved to have the snake (and us) out of the house.

We had no way of bringing this particular snake home, but because it was garbage day in town, we searched through several blue boxes until we found a large empty box of chocolates. The words 'Get Well Soon' were written across the top of the bright red box.

"Perfect," said Paulo, and we pedaled back to find our snake still sitting on the rock where we had left him.

We spent the rest of the day showing the snake to our mothers, first mine, then Paulo's, and finally Gordon's. Her reaction was better than we expected. She yelled, "Gordon, how many times do I have to tell you that you can't keep a pet snake?" Seeing the 'sad looks' on our faces, she added in a softer voice, "If you get rid of the snake, I'll take you boys out for ice cream. Just let the snake go in the woods, and we'll all go get a chocolate sundae later."

"Well, OK," sighed Gordon, and we biked happily away.

"Hey," said Gordon, before we had gone too far "I'm going to keep this snake and take it to school on Monday."

68

"What for?" asked Paulo.

"I'll show him to the other kids and then let him go in the woods behind the school."

"You'll have to be careful not to let the teachers see it, or you'll be in big trouble," I added.

"No problem," said Gordon. "The teachers will never even know it was there."

Hmmm, I thought to myself. *Gordon, a snake, and a school yard full of kids. What could possibly go wrong?*

Gordon hid the snake from his mother all weekend, and on Monday morning he brought it to school in the red chocolate box to show the other kids in our class. When the bell rang, Gordon carefully snuck the red box, with the snake still coiled up inside it, into his desk, planning to let it go at recess. Returning from her week away, Mrs. Hoagsbrith made her way into the classroom, walking slowly and looking pale. Obviously, she was still not fully recovered from her recent operation.

Speaking quietly, Mrs. H. told us to take out our geography books, and when Gordon opened his desk, she saw the bright red chocolate box hidden inside.

"Gordon, what's in that box?" she asked curiously. Before Gordon could speak, Mrs. H. reached in and picked up the red box. She read out loud what was written on the top of the box: 'Get Well Soon.' A tear came to her eye and she sat down in her chair, clutching the box to her chest. Fighting back tears, she said, "In all my years of teaching, this is the nicest thing a class has ever done for me. All of you pitching in to buy me this get well box of chocolates! You are the best class a teacher could ever have! I'm just sorry I found it and spoiled your surprise."

Every kid in class held their breath. When Mrs. Hoagsbrith opened that box, we would all be in trouble, the kind of trouble that meant a phone call home to our parents, and we would suddenly become the *worst* class Mrs. H. had ever had. Our teacher sat the box down on her desk without opening it, and we all breathed a temporary sigh of relief.

"Getting me that gift was so nice that I'm cancelling all school work for today. Let's just go to the gym, have an extra recess, and then spend the rest of the day watching a couple of movies."

The entire day passed without Mrs. Hoagsbrith lifting the lid off the red box on her desk.

*   *   *   *   *

The next morning, we filed into the classroom expecting to be in big trouble. We were surprised to find our teacher still smiling happily at us.

Unable to stand the suspense any longer, Gordon raised his hand and cautiously asked, "Mrs. H., how were the chocolates?" And then it happened.

Mrs. Hoagsbrith frowned and looked a little sad. "Well, class. As much as I loved your thoughtfulness, I'm afraid I'm allergic to chocolate." Then her face brightened. "But don't worry. Your gift won't be wasted. My mother turns 90 years old on Friday, so I took the box of chocolates to the post office after work yesterday and mailed it to her for a big surprise!"

Chapter 9

Money, Money, Money!

Parents often tell their kids that money can't buy happiness but Gordon, Paulo and I know that isn't true. If money can't buy happiness, why do parents buy lottery tickets? Do they think winning a million dollars would make them *un*happy?

Gordon, Paulo and I currently had no money, and this was making us *very* unhappy. Fortunately, we got an opportunity for happiness that day. We were heading out on our bikes to see if we could find any cans and bottles that people had thrown into the ditch by the road, but we didn't get far. Gordon's neighbour, Mr. Butterworth, waved to us from the end of his driveway and said, "How would you boys like to make some money?"

We slammed on the brakes, leaving skid marks. Mr. Butterworth continued. "You see," he said, pointing to a big heap on his driveway, "I had a load of sheep manure delivered for my garden, but they delivered twice as much as I wanted. My sister only lives about twenty minutes away, and she said she'd like the extra manure for her garden. I'm too old to run this stuff back and forth, but I'll pay you boys twenty dollars each to deliver it for me. It should only take about five trips."

Gordon, Paulo and I quickly agreed. "But how will we deliver it?" asked Gordon. "Should we get our old wagons?"

"Oh, no," said Mr. Butterworth. "I just bought a brand new wheelbarrow that you can use. Mind you, I want you to take good care of it. It cost me sixty bucks."

Mr. Butterworth returned to his house, and we got to work. We took turns shoveling the sheep manure into the wheelbarrow, and when we had a full load, we wheeled it over to Mr. Butterworth's sister's house. It was hot, smelly, dirty work, but it was worth it for twenty dollars each!

We had just completed our fourth trip when Gordon looked longingly at a restaurant that we had passed on each of our rounds. "Man, I'm starving," he said. "When we get paid, the first thing I'm going to do is come back here for a big meal and an even bigger drink!"

"Me, too," I agreed.

"Let's hurry, then," said Paulo. "I think we can finish this job in one more trip."

As we were shoveling the last of the sheep manure into Mr. Butterworth's new wheelbarrow, the old man came out of his house.

"I have to go out, but first I want to pay you boys and thank you for a job well done. You've worked hard, and you deserve this money." He handed each of us a twenty dollar bill. "Now don't spend it until the all the work is done."

"Thanks! We won't," we promised.

"Just put the wheelbarrow in the shed and lock the door when you're all done," said Mr. Butterworth as he got into his car and headed off, leaving Gordon, Paulo and me to finish the job. When the last of the manure was in the wheelbarrow, we took off one last time. It was an especially heavy load, and by the time we reached the restaurant, we were thirstier and hungrier than ever.

"Why don't we stop for something to eat and drink right now," said Gordon. "We have the money Mr. Butterworth gave us, and then we'll have more energy to deliver this last load."

"I don't know," said Paulo. "We promised to finish the job and return the wheelbarrow first before we spent the money."

"Yeah," I agreed. "And what'll we do with this load of manure if we stop for a break now?"

"We'll leave it outside the restaurant," said Gordon. "Who's gonna steal manure? And besides, Mr. Butterworth will never even know."

Gordon was right. No one was going to steal a pile of useless, stinky manure! "Let's go eat!" I agreed.

We parked the load of manure outside the restaurant and went in, confident that the manure would still be there when we returned.

Half an hour later we emerged from the restaurant to finish the job. And then it happened. Just as Gordon had predicted, no one had stolen the manure. However, it was dumped on the sidewalk, and someone had stolen Mr. Butterworth's brand new $60.00 wheelbarrow!!

Chapter 10

When Aliens Attack!

It was Friday after school and Gordon and I decided, for once, to get our homework done early so that we could enjoy the rest of the weekend. Gordon suddenly threw down his pencil and said, "Did you ever notice that when a kid makes a mistake, the teacher always says, 'Keep trying. Practice makes perfect'?"

"Yeah. So what?" I asked.

"And," continued Gordon. "Did you ever notice that when the teacher makes a mistake, she says, 'Nobody's perfect'?"

"Yeah. So what?" I said again.

"Well, if practice makes perfect, but nobody's perfect, I say, there's no sense wasting time practising!"

As usual, Gordon was right. We closed our books and decided to head over to Paulo's house to see what he was up to. Biking over to the farm, we expected to see Paulo doing his regular farm chores, but when we got to the barn, we were surprised to see a large truck hidden inside. Paulo and his dad were busy unloading tables and chairs from the back of the truck and stacking them out of sight behind bales of hay. On the side of the truck was a sign that said:

El Cheapo's Party Truck

**Everything you need to throw your next
Anniversary, Wedding or Birthday Party.
Why Pay a Professional Caterer Big $$
When You Can *Do It Yourself* and
Save Big $$**

Noticing Gordon and me standing in the barn, Mr. Lima said, "Hurry! Close the barn door!" Then, breaking into a big grin, he added, "How nice to see two of my favourite boys! I'm so glad you're here."

Mr. Lima was a hardworking man who didn't usually waste time talking to us kids, and getting a compliment from him was rare. Gordon and I beamed with pleasure.

Mr. Lima continued. "My, what strong arm muscles you two are getting!"

"Thank you," we said, flexing our biceps.

Mr. Lima stepped a bit closer. "My, what strong shoulder muscles you two are getting!"

Gordon and I grinned and stood up taller.

Mr. Lima leaned forward and said, "Your backs! What strong looking backs you have!"

By now, Gordon and I were getting a little embarrassed by all the compliments, but before we could say anything, Mr. Lima reached out and grabbed each of us by the arm. Pulling us towards the truck, he said, "And all the better to help Paulo and me unload this big truck!"

The next thing we knew, Gordon and I were put to work lugging heavy tables, chairs and boxes off the truck. As we worked, Paulo explained to us that his dad was throwing a big surprise party for Mrs. Lima's 40th birthday, but when he found out how much professional caterers charged, he decided to save some money by doing it himself – himself meaning with the help of Gordon, Paulo and me.

While we sweated away, Mr. Lima said, "Any fool can throw a party. Why pay expensive professionals when I can do everything myself and save big money?" I guess he decided it was time to give us a little man-to-man talk because he continued on as the three of us worked. "You see, boys, life isn't all fun and games. One day you're going to wake up and find yourself married with children, and you're going to have to learn the value of a dollar. The professionals wanted to charge me thousands of dollars to set up this party, and even though I could afford it, I did it myself for only a few hundred bucks. I want you to remember one thing – a fool and his money soon part. Do you understand what that means?"

"Yeah. Sure," we grunted as we lugged the last of the heavy objects off the truck.

"To thank you for all your hard work, here is $10.00 for each of you," said Mr. Lima, reaching into his wallet and taking out three bills.

"Thanks!" said Gordon. "Quick, guys. Grab your bikes and let's hurry to town to spend our money!!"

Rolling his eyes, Mr. Lima said, "Wait! Just one more thing. I'm taking Mrs. Lima out for dinner tonight. I want her to think that's all she's getting for her birthday – a special dinner at a French restaurant. That way, she'll be really surprised by the party tomorrow night. So while I'm gone, I need you boys to finish getting ready for the party. I've rented a big tank of helium and bought a thousand balloons and some twinkle lights. They're up in the loft." The three of us looked up. "I want you to fill all the balloons, tie a twinkle light to each one, and then tie the strings to the railing so they won't float away. Tomorrow night, I'll decorate the entire farm with the balloons and when it gets dark, the twinkle lights will automatically turn on. It will be beautiful. Do you think you boys can handle the job?"

Hmmm, I thought. *Three boys, a farm, and a tank of helium. What could possibly go wrong?* Then a crazy vision popped into my head: Pigs, cows and chickens somehow inhaling the helium, blowing up like balloons and floating off. I shook the vision away.

Gordon, Paulo and I promised Mr. Lima that we could be trusted to get the job done. The Lima's left for their fancy dinner, and we got to work. We worked as quickly as we could, filling the balloons and tying a twinkle light onto each one. Then we tied the strings to the railing of the loft to keep them from floating away, just like Mr. Lima had told us. It was dark by the time we finished filling the thousand balloons.

"Well, that's it," I said at last. "Time to head home."

"Not so fast," said Gordon, eyeing the large tank of helium. "I think there's still some helium left."

"And look," I said, pointing. "There's a whole box of balloons left over, and lots of twinkle lights. I think your dad ordered too much stuff, Paulo."

"I'll let him know so he can return it for a refund," Paulo said.

"What!" cried Gordon. "Tell your dad? Why, that's crazy talk! It would just upset him to know that he wasted his money buying too much stuff. Remember all that talk about 'a fool and his money'? We don't want to embarrass him by letting him know how much more money he could have saved. No, the thing to do is to fill up these balloons, tie on the extra lights, and float them away. That way, he'll never know just how much money he could have saved."

"I guess you're right," agreed Paulo. "I wouldn't want to make my dad feel like a fool."

"You're absolutely right," said Gordon. "For gosh sakes, your dad's self-esteem is at stake here!"

Paulo and I grinned at each other. No one could twist wrong into right faster than Gordon, and we quickly got to work filling the extra balloons. When we were finished, we had hundreds of balloons, each tied to a tiny twinkle light. We grabbed them and carried them outside. Away from the bright light of the barn, the little lights automatically began twinkling, and instantly, the dark night was filled with beautiful coloured blinking lights. On the count of three, we let go of the strings, and the balloons floated up and away. The balloons disappeared from sight, and all we could see was the night sky filling up with hundreds of tiny, flashing twinkle lights floating harmlessly away.

*   *   *   *   *

Every year in June, our town holds a Children's Festival, and tonight, it was well underway. Hundreds of families had headed out to the park to hear music, stories, and dancing. When it grew dark, families gathered on blankets to enjoy a concert, and as they sat, listening to the music, an odd sight began filling the sky from the west. And then it happened. At first it went unnoticed, but as the pleasant breeze swept across the park, it carried with it hundreds of balloons, each attached to a tiny twinkle light.

Spying the flashing lights heading straight towards them, a little boy pointed and shouted, "Look!" Instantly all eyes went to the sky overhead, which was now filled with hundreds of mysterious flashing lights. In our town, mysterious flashing lights in the sky can mean only one thing: UFOs!! Several of the balloons got tangled in the branches of the tall trees, causing the lights to hover directly overhead. The music stopped, and nervous parents rushed to pick up their children.

Hoping to avoid a panic, the mayor jumped up onto the stage, grabbed a microphone and said, "Men, now is the time to be brave! Come with me and we'll see if there is any real danger here." The next instant, several of the balloons that were caught in the trees began to explode! "But first," shouted the mayor, "we must lead the women and children to safety!" and with that, the mayor and the men bravely ran away, leading the path to safety. Women and children followed, racing after their brave husbands and fathers.

Parked under a bridge not far from the park were two of our town's police officers. Sergeants Roswell and Fido were on duty keeping our town safe from danger when they were startled awake by a flash mob of screaming men, women and children racing past their patrol car. Nothing bothered Sergeant Roswell and Sergeant Fido more than a flash mob of screaming citizens disturbing their naps. They stepped out of the car and held up their hands. "STOP!" commanded Sergeant Fido. "What's going on?" The crowd continued to thunder past them, but several people turned and pointed into the sky behind them. "Aliens! In the park!! Shooting!" they yelled.

Both policemen looked up and saw the mysterious blinking lights and heard the "shots" as more balloons became entangled in the trees and popped. With more than thirty years of experience, the officers knew exactly what to do. "RUN!" they shouted. "Run for your lives!" Pushing Sergeant Rowell back into the patrol car, Sergeant Fido gunned the engine. Gravel flew out from under the spinning tires as the policemen raced to safety.

Reaching the edge of town, the sergeant reached forward and pushed a button on the dashboard of the car that said, 'MILITARY DEFENSE. CONTACT IN EVENT OF NATIONAL EMERGENCY ONLY.' Immediately a calm voice came over the radio. "National Air Defense. Please state the nature of the emergency."

"Aliens!" shouted Sergeant Fido. "Our town's thick with 'em!! Send help right away!!" The sergeant sat back in his seat, relieved and pleased with himself for a job well done. Turning to his partner, he explained that he was going to hide out in his cabin in the woods for a few days to wait things out. "We must protect ourselves so that we can bring law and order back to the town in case anyone survives."

"Sounds like a great plan," said Sergeant Roswell.

*   *   *   *   *

No one takes alien fighting more seriously than the military. Secret spy satellites immediately locked onto our town and confirmed that it was indeed surrounded by unidentified flying objects. The General in charge demanded to know what direction the aliens had come from.

"Sir!" a lieutenant answered. "Tracking shows that the aliens launched their attack four kilometers west of town, from what appears to be a large barn, sir."

"So," replied the General, rubbing his hands together. "Those sneaky aliens think they can build a secret UFO airbase and disguise it as a barn, do they? Well, not while I'm in charge! Lieutenant, blow up that alien airbase immediately!"

"Uh, sir," gulped the lieutenant. "Shouldn't we confirm that the target is an actual alien airbase first and not just some cow barn *before* we blow it up, sir?"

"Okay, Mr. Alien-Lover," sighed the General. "You can take your team and check things out, but don't blame me if you get abducted by aliens! Come back and give me a full report, if you survive. *Then* we'll blow it up!"

*   *   *   *   *

Meanwhile, back at the barn, Gordon, Paulo and I had decided to call it a night. As we were closing and locking the barn doors, we heard a strange sound off in the distance. It quickly grew to a roar and the sky was instantly filled with dozens of military helicopters beaming blinding searchlights directly down on us. With a rush of wind that felt like a hurricane, they began landing all around us – in the pasture, in the middle of the fields where crops and fences were instantly flattened, and in Paulo's mother's prized flower beds. We watched in horrified silence as soldiers leapt from the machines and quickly fanned out all over the farm. Four soldiers dressed all in black ran over to Gordon, Paulo and me, and one shouted, "You three! On

the ground! Hands behind your head and don't move!"
Gordon, Paulo and I were confused. Was he talking to us?
Before we could ask, we were slammed to the ground, a
heavy combat boot resting on each of our backs. I realized
now that yes, he had been talking to us.

I heard the man talking into his radio. "Farm is secure.
Nothing here but three stupid looking kids."

Curious, I popped my head up to see what kids had
arrived at the farm. Instantly, I felt a combat boot pressed
against the back of my head, reminding me that I wasn't
supposed to move. *Man,* I thought as my face was pressed
into the dirt. *I sure hope our teachers never find out how
well this works.*

Once the soldiers were satisfied that this wasn't a secret
alien airbase, Gordon, Paulo and I were allowed to stand
up. Brushing ourselves off, we saw a car turning into the
laneway. Paulo's parents were back from their dinner!
Instantly, their car was surrounded by soldiers. Paulo's dad
was asked to step out of the car and show his ID. Then,
with his hands on his head, he was patted down by one of
the soldiers. Darting his eyes around his farm, he took in

the broken fences, damaged crops and the cows milling about everywhere. I heard him say, "My farm! *Those boys!!* I trusted those boys and my farm is destroyed!"

"Uh-oh," whispered Gordon. "This looks serious. Do you think he's gonna want his $10.00 back?"

"I'm not waiting around to find out!" I hissed back.

Deciding it was best to let the adults sort things out, Gordon, Paulo and I snuck away and grabbed our bikes. We headed straight to town as quickly as we could pedal. When we were a safe distance away, Gordon said, "Wow, your dad really messed things up big time!"

"My dad?" said Paulo. "How do you figure *he* messed things up?"

"He trusted us!" said Gordon. "I mean, what responsible adult would leave a bunch of boys in charge of anything? I'm really disappointed in him."

Paulo and I nodded our heads in agreement. "Yes," I said. "It was very poor parenting, indeed."

"All this trouble because he was too cheap to hire a caterer!" said Gordon. "I guess poor Mr. Lima never heard the expression, *'you get what you pay for'.*"